D1453715

STATES OF MIND

I FEEL ANXIOUS

BY ABBY COOPER

BLUE OWL
BOOKS

TIPS FOR CAREGIVERS

Social and emotional learning (SEL) helps children manage emotions, create and achieve goals, maintain relationships, learn how to feel empathy, and make good decisions. The SEL approach will help children establish positive habits in communication, cooperation, and decision-making. By incorporating SEL in early reading, children will be better equipped to build confidence and foster positive peer networks.

BEFORE READING

Talk to the reader about noticing anxiety. Explain that everyone feels it sometimes.

Discuss: Have you ever felt worried? What are some things you have felt worried about? How do you think feeling worried and feeling anxious are the same? What about excitement?

AFTER READING

Talk to the reader about the way anxiety makes us feel and act.

Discuss: What are some signs and symptoms of anxiety? Does it impact the way you think and feel? What can you do if you feel anxious?

SEL GOAL

Anxiety is common and impacts many people of all ages. While it can feel similar to excitement, anxiety is usually defined as a feeling of extreme worry or unease. Some students may struggle with anxiety but not know how to express their anxious thoughts or feelings. Help them find words for their feelings and inner experiences.

TABLE OF CONTENTS

CHAPTER 1

WHAT IS ANXIETY?

Sophie is about to speak in front of her class. Her heart pounds. Her body feels hot. She has butterflies in her stomach. She feels both excited and nervous.

There is a good chance Sophie also feels **anxious**. Anxiety is feeling very **uneasy**. It happens when we are facing an uncertain outcome. Will Sophie's speech be a success? Or will it flop?

Do your worries feel like they never end? Or are they a bigger deal than they should be? If so, you are probably feeling anxious.

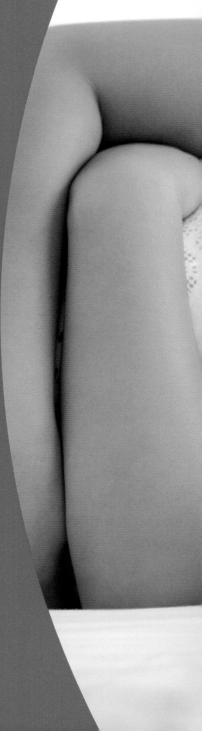

ANXIETY VS. EXCITEMENT

Anxiety is often confused with nervousness or excitement. These feelings are a lot alike. But nerves and excitement fade away. Anxiety sticks around. It can be much harder to control.

bee

Anxiety can be different for everyone. It can be short-term or ongoing. Many **factors** cause anxiety. It can run in families. It can also be the result of an event. Becca was stung by a bee. Now just seeing one makes her feel anxious. Her heart beats fast.

GOOD ANXIETY

Everybody feels anxious sometimes. Some people like it and seek it out! Why? The **adrenaline** our bodies makes gives us **energy**! This can happen when we watch scary movies or ride roller coasters.

CHAPTER 2

WHAT IT LOOKS AND FEELS LIKE

How can you know if you're feeling anxious? Look for clues in your body. Are you **fidgety** or **tense**?

A stomachache or a racing heart could be **symptoms** of anxiety. Your heartbeat may speed up, and it could be hard to catch your breath. Do you feel sweaty, dizzy, or like you may get sick?

Bodies react in many ways. Identify how anxiety feels in your body. Symptoms occur in your mind, too. What are your thoughts like? Identifying your thoughts and symptoms is the first step toward controlling anxious feelings.

While it is normal and OK to feel anxious, anxiety becomes a problem when it is **excessive**. Luckily, there are many ways to **cope** with these feelings.

CHAPTER 3

HOW TO COPE

Start with your body. Eat well, exercise, and get enough sleep. These all help clear your mind.

Writing or drawing in a journal helps, too. It is important to **express** how you feel. Journaling can help you organize your thoughts and feel in control of your feelings.

journal

Another way to cope is to practice deep breathing. This is one of the best ways to reduce **stress**. If your heart starts to race, try this. Breathe in deep through your nose. Hold it for a few seconds. Then let it out. Breathing sends a message to your brain to calm down.

POSITIVE SELF-TALK

Use **positive self-talk**. Remind yourself that you are safe and loved. Reframe any negative thoughts. Instead of, "I will never get all of my work done," try, "I will do my best and ask for help if I need it."

If someone you know feels anxious, you can help by listening. Don't tell your friend to relax or calm down. Avoid saying a worry is silly. This could make the anxiety worse. Instead, remind your friend that his or her feelings are OK. Simply being there for your friend can make a huge difference.

counselor

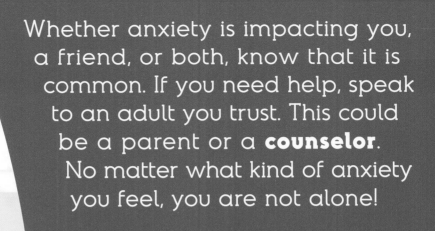

Whether anxiety is impacting you, a friend, or both, know that it is common. If you need help, speak to an adult you trust. This could be a parent or a **counselor**. No matter what kind of anxiety you feel, you are not alone!

GOALS AND TOOLS

GROW WITH GOALS

Notice when you feel anxious. Try these strategies to help.

Goal: Be mindful! Breathe slowly and deeply. Identify something around you with each of your 5 senses. Paying attention to your body instead of your racing thoughts can help you relax.

Goal: Change the story! Identify thoughts that make you feel anxious. Replace them with positive thoughts that are helpful.

Goal: Let it out! Write or draw your thoughts and feelings in a journal. Then share them with a friend or an adult you trust.

TRY THIS!

When you're feeling anxious, it can be hard to calm down. That's why it's helpful to prepare before it happens. Make a Calm Kit so you'll be ready when anxiety strikes.

1. Find a bin, basket, or box. Label it "Calm Kit."

2. Gather items that make you feel calm. These could include favorite toys, items, or photos of people, places, and things that make you feel safe and loved. These items could also include written reminders to yourself or supportive notes from family members, teachers, or friends.

3. Keep your Calm Kit somewhere where it is easy to find.

GLOSSARY

adrenaline
A chemical that your body produces when you need more energy or when you sense danger.

anxious
Worried or very eager to do something.

cope
To deal with something effectively.

counselor
Someone trained to help with problems or give advice.

energy
The ability or strength to do things without getting tired.

excessive
More than necessary.

express
To show what you feel or think with words, writing, or actions.

factors
Things that help produce a result.

fidgety
Moving because of nervousness, restlessness, or boredom.

positive self-talk
Words or thoughts to yourself that make you feel good about yourself and your abilities.

stress
Mental or emotional strain or pressure.

symptoms
Signs of something.

tense
Stretched stiff and tight.

uneasy
Worried, nervous, or anxious.

TO LEARN MORE

FACT SURFER

Finding more information is as easy as 1, 2, 3.

1. Go to www.factsurfer.com

2. Enter "**Ifeelanxious**" into the search box.

3. Choose your cover to see a list of websites.

INDEX

Blue Owl Books are published by Jump!, 5357 Penn Avenue South, Minneapolis, MN 55419, www.jumplibrary.com

Library of Congress Cataloging-in-Publication Data

Names: Cooper, Abby, author.
Title: I feel anxious / Abby Cooper.
Description: Minneapolis, MN: Jump!, Inc., [2021]
Series: States of mind | Includes index.
Audience: Ages 7–10 | Audience: Grades 2–3
Identifiers: LCCN 2019046336 (print)
LCCN 2019046337 (ebook)
ISBN 9781645273950 (hardcover)
ISBN 9781645273967 (paperback)
ISBN 9781645273974 (ebook)
Subjects: LCSH: Anxiety–Juvenile literature. | Emotions in children–Juvenile literature.
Classification: LCC BF575.A6 C66 2021 (print)
LCC BF575.A6 (ebook) | DDC 155.4/1246–dc23
LC record available at https://lccn.loc.gov/2019046336
LC ebook record available at https://lccn.loc.gov/2019046337

Editor: Jenna Gleisner
Designer: Molly Ballanger

Photo Credits: Krakenimages.com/Shutterstock, cover, 10; Ami Parikh/Shutterstock, 1; TinnaPong/Shutterstock, 3; Syda Productions/Shutterstock, 4, 5; bymuratdeniz/iStock, 6–7; kojihirano/iStock, 8–9; Daisy-Daisy/iStock, 11; Kalinovskiy/iStock, 12–13; Spotmatik Ltd/Shutterstock, 14; mg7/iStock, 15; YAKOBCHUK VIACHESLAV/Shutterstock, 16–17; monkeybusinessimages/iStock, 18–19; Antonio Diaz/Getty, 20–21.

Printed in the United States of America at Corporate Graphics in North Mankato, Minnesota.